THE ARISTOCATS

THE ARISTOCATS

Based on Walt Disney's
full-length animated movie

Adapted by Nigel Robinson

Hippo

Scholastic Children's Books,
Scholastic Publications Ltd,
7–9 Pratt Street, London NW1 0AE

Scholastic Inc.,
555 Broadway, New York, NY 10012-3999, USA

Scholastic Canada Ltd,
123 Newkirk Road, Richmond Hill,
Ontario, Canada L4C 3G5

Ashton Scholastic Pty Ltd,
P O Box 579, Gosford, New South Wales,
Australia

Ashton Scholastic Ltd,
Private Bag 92801, Penrose, Auckland,
New Zealand

First published by Scholastic Publications Ltd 1994
Text copyright © Walt Disney Ltd 1994

ISBN 0 590 55618 5

Typeset in Plantin by Contour Typesetters, Southall, London
Printed by Cox & Wyman, Reading, Berks

10 9 8 7 6 5 4 3 2 1

LIST OF COLOUR PLATES

1 Madame Adelaide strokes Duchess, her graceful white pedigree cat.

2 Edgar has just heard that Madame Adelaide is leaving him her vast fortune – after her cats have died.

3 Duchess teaches her kittens that they must grow up to be real Aristicats, and they learn their scales and arpeggios.

4 Edgar concocts a sleeping potion which he will feed to the Aristocats – he is determined to get rid of them.

5 Duchess and the kittens have been catnapped by Edgar, and wake up in the middle of nowhere.

6 On the opposite bank of the river stands a large ginger tom-cat – Thomas O'Malley, the alley cat.

7 The kittens lap milk from a churn as they travel in the back of a milk van to Paris.

8 Thomas, Duchess and the kittens hide underneath a train track as a train thunders past.

9 Back in Paris, Abigail and Amelia, the English geese, meet up with their Uncle Waldo.

1

A long time ago at the turn of the century, Madame Adelaide lived in a huge and magnificent mansion in the centre of Paris. The capital of France was then the most glamorous and stylish city in the world; and, of all the grand ladies in that town, Madame Adelaide was surely one of the grandest and most stylish.

When she was younger she had been a famous opera singer, stunning the crowds from Paris to London to Milan. Now she contented herself with strolling leisurely along the grand boulevards of the French capital, or just sitting in her expensive home where she listened to the recordings she had made when she was younger.

Madame Adelaide was no longer married, but she was far from being lonely. Many rich and influential friends came to visit her often, and she always had the company of her servants and her chief butler, Edgar.

But of all her friends, the ones she valued the most,

1

and whom she would not give up, even for the highest of all Parisian society, were her cats.

Of course, they weren't ordinary cats, you understand; not the sort you might see on a street corner, hanging around the garbage cans where the common cats played . . . No, these cats were pedigree cats, skilled in each and every one of the social graces. These elegant and sophisticated felines slept only on the finest velvet mats, and ate only the best food and milk.

After all, such luxury was only fitting for cats who resided at one of the finest addresses in all Paris. And it is no wonder that all the other cats in the neighbourhood called Madame Adelaide's cats by the only name which was appropriate. Madame Adelaide's cats were known simply as The Aristocats.

Frou-Frou the mare proudly pulled Madame's carriage through the cobbled streets of Paris, as all the other horses looked on enviously. They all wished that they too could work for Madame Adelaide, and Frou-Frou secretly enjoyed all the attention her fellow horses were giving her.

Behind her in the carriage sat Madame herself, stroking a tiny white kitten, who was purring in her lap. Sitting in front of Madame holding the reins was Edgar, the butler, who also served as Madame's coachman.

Madame continued to stroke the purring kitten, and cooed softly to her. "Ah, Marie," she sighed, "you're going to grow up to be as beautiful as your mother. Isn't she, Duchess?"

She looked over to Duchess who was sitting next to Madame; the tall and graceful white pedigree cat was gazing lovingly at her new kitten. Duchess gave a "meow" of agreement and then turned her attention to her other children, Toulouse, and Berlioz, who was riding at the front on Frou-Frou's back. She shook her head fondly: Berlioz was still little more than a kitten but there would have to come a time when he realized that riding on a horse's back was simply not the way a young Aristocat should behave!

As Edgar tugged on Frou-Frou's reins to turn her into Madame's street, Toulouse leapt onto the butler's shoulder and started to playfully lick the man's ear. Behind him, Madame laughed, but Edgar scowled and roughly picked the cat up by the scruff of the neck and deposited him on the wooden floor of the carriage. Toulouse shot him an annoyed look. Didn't he know that that was no way to treat an Aristocat?

Pulling up outside Madame's grand house, Edgar jumped down from the carriage and offered his hand to Madame to help her down. She picked up the purchases she had made that day from the most exclusive shops in Paris, and was about to enter the house, when she remembered something. She reached into her bag and took out a sugar lump, which she gave to Frou-Frou who chomped on it happily.

"May I take your parcel, Madame?" asked Edgar. "It's really much too heavy for you." He was always eager to please his employer. After all, she was a very rich woman and might remember poor old Edgar one day in her will.

Madame tut-tutted and walked past the butler. "Don't fuss over me!" she chided and walked past into the house.

While the two humans were talking, Duchess and her family jumped out of the carriage and began to walk smartly over to the house. Berlioz raced out in front, but was called back by his mother.

"Haven't you forgotten something, darling?" Duchess asked in a stern voice.

Berlioz shrugged and thought hard. He saw his mother glance over to Frou-Frou and then remembered his good manners. He scampered over to the horse.

"Thank you for letting me ride on your back, Miss Frou-Frou," he said politely.

Frou-Frou chuckled in a horsey way. "You're quite welcome, young man," she said.

Berlioz turned proudly to his mother. "Was that all right, Mama?" he asked.

"Very good," Duchess nodded approvingly.

"Come along, Duchess and kittens!" called

Madame, who was waiting for them at the door. As the cats walked through the grand door, Madame turned to Edgar who was just about to lead Frou-Frou to the stables at the back of the house.

"I'm expecting my lawyer, Georges Hautecourt, today," she informed him. "You remember him, of course."

Edgar sighed and raised his eyes to the heavens. "Of course, madame," he said. "How could anyone forget him?"

Madame's lawyer, Monsieur Hautecourt, acted like a young man of twenty-one. Unfortunately, he was over eighty, and as he drove up to Madame's house in his new-fangled motor car, elderly Parisian ladies looked on disapprovingly at the old man's antics.

Edgar was waiting for him at the door and invited him in. "Good day, sir," he said a little snootily. "Madame is expecting you."

Hautecourt skipped up the steps, and past Edgar. Then he did a little twirl and with the help of his cane, took his hat off his head and flipped it expertly over to the butler. It landed full-square on the butler's bald head.

"Well done, sir," said Edgar. "Another ringer—you never miss."

The eighty-year-old lawyer chuckled and raced over to the stairs.

"Come on, Edgar!" he said enthusiastically. "The last one up the stairs is a nincompoop!"

Edgar sighed again, more heavily this time. "Could we possibly take the elevator this time, sir?" he asked wearily.

"That birdcage?" Hautecourt scoffed and began to hobble up the stairs. "Elevators are for old people!"

Edgar refrained from mentioning the fact that Hautecourt wasn't exactly a spring-chicken himself, and followed him up the stairs to Madame's sitting room.

"Can I give you a hand, sir?" he enquired, as the old man hobbled up the stairs.

"You haven't got an extra foot, have you?" asked the lawyer and guffawed with laughter.

Edgar chuckled obediently. "That one always makes me laugh, sir," he said, even though it was at least the twentieth time this year that Hautecourt had cracked the same joke.

Madame was holding Duchess in her arms and stroking her as Edgar rapped on the door and announced Monsieur Hautecourt. At her feet, Marie, dressed in a pretty new pink ribbon, was playing while Berlioz and Toulouse were chasing each other in the far corner of the room.

"Announcing Monsieur Georges Hautecourt," Edgar said pompously, like a Master of Ceremonies at a grand charity ball, and Madame's old friend tottered into the room.

"Goodness, Edgar, I know who Georges is," Madame reproved. "It's so good to see you again, Georges."

Still holding Duchess in one arm, Madame held out her hand for her old friend to kiss.

"Adelaide, my dear," he said and bent down to kiss her hand. Instead, the short-sighted old man picked up Duchess's tail and kissed that!

"Ah, still the softest hands in all of Paris!" Hautecourt sighed, remembering the days of their youth when they had danced together all night celebrating Madame's performance in the opera, *Carmen*. In Madame's arms Duchess purred softly to herself.

Madame laughed at her old friend's mistake. "You're a shameless old flatterer!" she said, but she clearly enjoyed the attention.

Suddenly she put Duchess down on the floor, where she rejoined her kittens, and became serious. She led Hautecourt to her desk, on which there were already piled mountains of important-looking documents. Next to the desk there was a speaking tube which Madame used when she wanted to summon Edgar up from the kitchen.

"I've asked you to come here on a very important legal matter, Georges," she said.

Hautecourt rubbed his hands together in glee. "Splendid, splendid!" he cackled. "Who do you want me to sue?"

"I don't want you to sue anyone," she said, as Hautecourt sat down at the desk and put on his glasses. "I simply want to make my will."

The lawyer opened his briefcase and took out his pen and paper. There was nothing like a good will, he thought; it was only then that you found out who people really liked and who they had just been being polite to for all those years! He started to write.

"Who are the beneficiaries?" he asked, his pen poised.

"Well, as you know, I have no living relatives," Madame began. She looked down at her feet where Duchess, Marie, Toulouse and Berlioz were playing happily. "And naturally I do want my beloved cats to be cared for," she continued. "And certainly, no one can do this better than my faithful servant, Edgar ..."

Down below in the kitchen, Edgar was ironing his trousers when he heard his name being mentioned. He stopped ironing and rushed over to the speaking tube where he eavesdropped on Madame and Hautecourt's conversation.

Monsieur Hautecourt couldn't believe what he was hearing, "*Edgar?*" he said. "Adelaide, you mean to

8

say that you're leaving your vast fortune to Edgar? Everything you possess—your stocks and bonds, this mansion, your country château, your art treasures, your jewels . . ."

"No, no, no, Georges," Madame interrupted. "I'm leaving them to my cats!"

"*To your cats?*"

"That's right," she said. "I simply wish to have the cats inherit first. Then, at the end of their life span, my entire estate will revert to Edgar . . ."

Edgar, of course, had heard everything. His eyes popped out of his head and he rubbed his hands greedily as he thought of all the riches which could be his. No longer would he be a lowly butler, serving dinner to all the great and famous people who came to visit Madame Adelaide. Now he would be a millionaire, and be as good as them. He would wear the finest clothes, eat in the swankiest restaurants, and travel the world on his very own yacht!

Then he scowled, as he remembered the conditions of Madame's will.

"The cats inherit first, and then I come after the cats," he muttered to himself, and smashed his fist angrily into the palm of his other hand. "It's not fair," he whined, "it's not fair. Each cat will live about twelve years and I can't wait that long . . ."

Another even more disturbing thought occurred to

him. "A cat has nine lives," he realised. "That's four times twelve and then multiply by nine times . . ." He tried to work out the calculation on his fingers and, when he couldn't, walked over to the ironing board and started to pull on his trousers. "Well, anyway, it's much longer than I'd ever live," he decided. "I'll be gone . . ."

An evil look came over the butler's face. "No, *they'll* be gone," he chuckled. "I'll think of a way to get rid of them . . ."

For a minute he was struck by a feeling of remorse. After all, what had Madame's cats ever done to harm him? Then he shook his head: he couldn't afford to miss out on his big chance now!

"There are millions of reasons why I should do it," he decided, and his eyes gleamed as he thought of spending all that money. "*Millions—millions* of dollars! *Those cats have got to go!*"

2

After Monsieur Hautecourt had left, Duchess and her three kittens retired to the salon of the house. Duchess was determined that Toulouse, Berlioz and Marie were going to grow up into real Aristocats, and would often bring her children here to practise their scales and arpeggios on Madame's very own fine grand piano.

Duchess's plans, however, fell apart when all three of her kittens tried to enter the salon through the catflap at the same time. The catflap was too small for all three of them and, as none of them would give an inch, they ended up getting stuck in the flap.

"Me first!" cried Marie, as she wriggled in between her two brothers, trying to squeeze herself through the catflap.

Toulouse sneered. "Why should you be first?" he demanded, peevishly.

Marie looked down her nose at him. "Because I'm a lady, that's why," she said sniffily.

11

"You're not a lady," said Toulouse, as Marie managed to squeeze past him. Berlioz pounced on her and grabbed her tail with his paw, bringing her down to the floor.

"You're nothing but a *sister!*" he laughed, and he and his brother sprang past her and into the room.

Marie was dazed. She was still very young and wasn't quite sure exactly what a *sister* was; but, as she picked herself up off the floor, she knew that she wasn't going to let Toulouse and Berlioz get the better of her.

"I'll show you if I'm a lady or not!" she cried and ran after the other two kittens.

A frantic romp followed as the three kittens chased each other around the salon. They would hide from each other behind pieces of antique furniture, ready to spring on each other when the other kitten least expected it.

Berlioz pounced on Marie, bringing her to the ground once more, and started to tickle her. Marie giggled with glee and then grabbed at the red ribbon around her brother's neck, pulling him down to the ground too.

"Fight fair, Marie," laughed Berlioz as the two of them rolled around on Madame's expensive Turkish carpet, almost knocking over an expensive floor vase.

"Huh!" said Toulouse, who was perched on top of

a candelabrum on a nearby table. "*Females* never fight fair!"

Suddenly the candelabrum began to sway, and Tolouse leapt off it before it could topple over. However, it was too late to stop one of the candles falling out and crashing down on Marie's head with a sickening *ker-plunk*!

The little kitten yelped in pain, and for a second Toulouse and Berlioz were worried. They had only planned on a spot of rough-and-tumble fun with their new baby sister; they certainly hadn't meant to hurt her. Luckily, Marie was more surprised than hurt, but she rose on her haunches and hissed at her two enemies.

At that moment Duchess strode in through the door, looking every inch a lady. She took in the scene at a glance: Marie, with half a broken candle on her head, Toulouse and Berlioz with their fur, which she had spent such a long time grooming and preening, now dishevelled and untidy.

"Marie, darling, you must not behave like this," Duchess tutted as she walked over to the nearest chair and sat on its velvet cushion. "This is really not lady-like . . ."

Toulouse and Berlioz chuckled silently to themselves, until Duchess turned to Berlioz and reprimanded him as well.

"And such behaviour is most unbecoming

to a lovely gentleman!"

Berlioz started to sulk. "Well, she started it," he lied, nodding over at his sister.

Marie jumped on the chair to join her mother, and looked down at Berlioz. "Ladies do not start fights," she said haughtily, and then added threateningly: "But they can *finish* them!"

In response, Berlioz stuck his tongue out at Marie.

"Berlioz!" reproved his mother. "Don't be rude!"

How was she ever going to teach her children to behave like proper ladies and gentlemen if they persisted in behaving like common cats fighting in an alley somewhere?

Berlioz shrugged, and continued to sulk. "We were just practising biting and clawing," he said, by way of an explanation.

"Aristocats do not practise biting and clawing," Duchess said sternly.

Toulouse, who had been listening to the conversation, jumped off the table (thankfully not upsetting another candlestick), and sprang to his brother's defence.

"But someday we might meet a tough alleycat!" he argued.

Duchess shuddered. The thought was almost too horrible to contemplate: she certainly didn't want her children mixing with *that* sort of common cat!

"Now that will do," she said, and then couldn't

help but laugh as Berlioz and Toulouse pawed at the air, pretending to be as rough and tough as streetwise alleycats. "It's time we concerned ourselves with self-improvement." She fixed her kittens with a serious stare. "You all want to grow up to be lovely and charming ladies and gentlemen, don't you?"

Marie, Toulouse and Berlioz looked at each other as if they weren't quite sure.

"Toulouse, you go and start your painting," said Duchess and nodded towards the easel in the corner of the room, at which Madame occasionally worked. Obediently, Toulouse trotted over to the easel.

Marie and Berlioz followed him after Duchess had given them permission to watch before they started their own music lesson at Madame's grand piano. They chuckled as they recognised the face of the person Tolouse was painting.

"It's old Pickle Puss, Edgar!" said Berlioz gleefully.

Duchess pretended to look shocked but couldn't help giggling at her children's name for the sour-faced butler.

"Now, now, Berlioz," she said as the kitten rolled on the floor in fits of laughter. "That is not kind!"

In fact Duchess found it hard not to laugh herself. She began to chuckle. "You know that Edgar is so fond of all of us, and he takes very good care of us . . ."

If she could have seen what Edgar was doing at that moment, Duchess would have revised her opinion of the old retainer. Indeed, she would have fled the house with her kittens immediately, in fear of her very life.

Down in the kitchen Edgar was hunched over the stove, stirring a pan of boiling milk. He was cackling away to himself and, if anyone had been watching, they would have been reminded of a witch crouched over her cauldron.

"Oh Edgar, you sly old fox!" he said to himself as he emptied the entire contents of a bottle of sleeping tablets into the pan, and continued to stir until they had all dissolved. Then he poured the sleeping potion into four fine-china bowls and placed them on a silver tray.

He left the kitchen and, careful not to spill a drop, started to climb the stairs which led to the salon.

All the time he sang a merry little tune to himself: "Bye, kitties, bye you go—and then Edgar's in the dough!"

Very soon Duchess and her three children would be no more—and Edgar the butler would be a millionaire!

16

The kittens, who had been practising a Mozart concerto on Madame's grand piano, stopped as soon as Edgar entered the salon, and slinked down to the floor. It wouldn't do, after all, for Edgar to suspect that they weren't just ordinary cats, but Aristocats. They mewed hungrily as Edgar approached with his silver tray laden with four bowls of hot milk.

"Good evening, my little ones," Edgar smirked as he laid the tray down on the floor. "Here's your favourite dish—prepared in a *very* special way!"

Duchess and her three children all licked their lips as they gathered around the four bowls; the smell of the hot creamy milk was too good to resist. That was one thing you could always rely on Madame for, thought Duchess: the very best food any Aristocat could ever dream of!

"It's crème de la crème à la Edgar!" the butler announced and turned to leave the Aristocats to their supper. As he left the room, he glanced behind him guiltily to see the four cats eagerly lapping up the milk.

"Sleep well," he said and then hastily corrected himself: "I mean, er, eat well, of course!"

As soon as Edgar had left the salon, the four cats heard a tiny squeaking noise from the other side of the room. They looked up from their milk and grinned as the tiny grey face of Roquefort, the mouse, peeped out from a hole in the skirting board.

He sniffed the delicious smell of warm milk coming from the cats' feeding bowls, and briefly popped back into his hole, only to appear a few seconds later carrying a half-eaten cracker.

Scampering boldly up to Duchess and her three children, he greeted each of them in turn. Marie, Toulouse, and Berlioz each returned his greeting politely, as they had been brought up to do.

That was the nice thing about this family, thought Roquefort. Normally cats and mice were deadly enemies, but Duchess and her children weren't like any old tom cat you might meet in the street. No sir, thought Roquefort gratefully, these cats had class!

"Good evening, Monsieur Roquefort," said Duchess, and Roquefort made a courtly bow. His nose twitched again at the delightful smell coming from the four bowls of milk.

"Something smells awfully good," he said, meaningfully. "What is that appetising smell?"

"It's crème de la crème à la Edgar," explained Marie, and drank a little more of the milk.

"Won't you join us, Monsieur Roquefort?" asked Duchess pleasantly.

"Well, I didn't mean . . ." flustered Roquefort, knowing that Duchess had guessed precisely what he had meant. "But it does so happen that I do have a cracker with me . . ."

"C'mon, Roquefort," chirped up Berlioz, and

moved away from his bowl slightly to make room for the tiny mouse. "Have some!"

Roquefort licked his lips and dunked his cracker into the bowl of milk. He nibbled on the biscuit: the milk tasted delicious.

"My compliments to the chef," he burped and took another bite of the cracker. "This is double delicious!"

Very soon Roquefort had eaten the whole of his cracker. He jumped off the tray and ran back to his mousehole for another biscuit as the four cats continued lapping up the milk.

Berlioz began to yawn, and by his side even the normally boisterous Toulouse was also feeling sleepy.

As soon as Roquefort reached his hole, he too started to yawn. The world seemed to be spinning dizzily around him as he turned to see Duchess, Marie, Berlioz and Toulouse all collapse on the floor, fast asleep.

Suddenly everything became clear to the tiny mouse. "So that's crème de la crème à la Edgar!" he realised before he too slumped to the floor, unconscious.

3

It was pitch-black as Edgar sneaked out of the back door of Madame's house and walked over to the stable where he kept his motorbike.

It was the middle of the night and there wasn't a sound to be heard; or at least there wasn't until Edgar tripped over a garbage can which fell clattering to the cobblestoned ground. He looked up at Madame's bedroom window, frightened that she might have been woken up by the noise. But in her bed Madame was sleeping soundly as though nothing untoward was happening.

Satisfied that he hadn't been discovered, Edgar tip-toed over to his motorbike. He was carrying a large wicker basket which he placed in the motorbike's side-car. As he did so, he lifted the cover of the basket and grinned: inside the basket, Duchess and her three children were still fast asleep. By the time they awoke they would be miles away from Paris, and Edgar would have Madame's millions all to himself!

For a second Toulouse opened his eyes, and saw Edgar standing over him. That was OK, he reasoned; after all, hadn't his mother said that Edgar was very fond of them all? He turned over and went back to sleep.

Sniggering evilly to himself, he climbed on the bike and roared noisily off into the dark Parisian night.

Very soon, the narrow winding roads of Paris gave way to the rough and bumpy pathways of the open countryside. Edgar breathed a sigh of relief: in Paris he had been scared in case anyone had stopped him. After all, a butler driving a motorbike with four pedigree cats in the back so late at night, might just raise suspicion. But here, in the open countryside, with only the stars for company, there was no one to spy on him.

At least that's what he thought; and once again he was proved wrong. As he drove past a deserted old windmill on the banks of the River Seine, the noise from his motorbike awoke a mangy old dog who was asleep underneath a broken-down hay-cart. He jumped up, hitting his head on the bottom of the cart, and then listened. He grinned: there was no mistaking that put-put-put sound! He was going to have some fun tonight!

He bounded over to a nearby haystack, from out of which popped the head of another dog.

"Hey, Lafayette!" began the first dog.

Lafayette shook the sleep out of his eyes, and the hay off his head. He grunted a sleepy "hello" to his friend, whose name was Napoleon.

"Listen!" said Napoleon as the sound of Edgar's motorbike came closer. "Wheels approaching!"

Lafayette sighed wearily. "Napoleon, we've done bit six tyres today," he protested. "We've chased four motorcars, and a bicycle, and a scooter . . ."

It sometimes seemed that Napoleon's one purpose in life was to chase as many vehicles as possible on this quiet country road. At this moment, all Lafayette wanted to do was to go back to sleep.

"Hush your mouth!" said Napoleon, and urged his companion to listen more closely. Edgar's motorbike was getting nearer and nearer.

In spite of himself, Lafayette came up and joined Napoleon, who was now lying in wait at the side of the road. In the distance they could see the tiny figure of Edgar approaching on the bike.

"It's a motorcycle!" said Napoleon and listened more carefully. "Two cylinders, a chain drive, one squeaky wheel on the front . . ."

Lafayette was genuinely impressed. When it came to motorbikes, there was no greater expert than Napoleon. Edgar was now so close that the two dogs could even see the covered basket in the side-car. Napoleon looked over at Lafayette.

"Now you go for the tyres," he whispered, and

22

then licked his lips. "And I'll go right for the seat of the problem!"

Lafayette snorted. "How come you always grab the tender part for yourself?" he asked grumpily.

"'Cause I outrank you, that's why!" replied Napoleon. Edgar was almost level with them now. "Stop beating your gums and sound the attack!"

Lafayette nodded and let out a blood-curdling howl. In the darkness, Edgar couldn't see where the sound was coming from; but he imagined it was from something very nasty indeed.

"OK!" said Lafayette. "Let's charge!" He began to race towards Edgar's motorbike when Napoleon slammed a paw down on his tail.

"Wait a minute!" he said. "I'm the leader! I'm the one that says when we go!"

Lafayette glowered at him.

"OK," said Napoleon. "Here we go!"

Barking and yelping, the two dogs raced towards the approaching motorbike.

Edgar shrieked in horror as he saw what he imagined to be two mad dogs charging straight towards him. He tried desperately to turn the bike right around, but he was going too fast and all he could manage to do was to veer off to the left.

Out of control now, the bike tumbled down the steep embankment leading to the river. Edgar hung on for his life as Napoleon and Lafayette, by now thoroughly enjoying themselves, ran after him.

As the bike bounced and bumped over the rough and rocky ground, the basket containing Duchess and her sleeping kittens was flung out of the side-car and landed in the mud on the river bank, underneath a bridge.

Edgar didn't notice that he no longer had the basket. All he was concerned about now was saving his own skin. He rode the bike along the embankment and even in the shallow waters of the river, but still Napoleon and Lafayette pursued him. The two dogs were having the time of their lives: they hadn't had such great fun in a long time!

They leapt into the sidecar and started snapping at the seat of Edgar's trousers. Edgar shrieked, and jumped onto the handlebars of the still-moving motorbike. Napoleon snapped at him once again.

"Nice doggy!" Edgar cried. "Nice doggy!"

Napoleon had never been called a "nice doggy" in his life and he certainly didn't want it to start now. He bit furiously at Edgar's trousers, ripping a huge chunk from his seat to reveal the butler's striped long-johns.

Furiously the butler tried to beat off the dog with his umbrella, but to no avail. In the struggle his hat fell off his head into the river, and was soon followed by his umbrella.

The motorbike was heading straight for a tree. Edgar closed his eyes as they hit the tree, the bike flying off in one direction and the side-car carrying Napoleon and Lafayette in the other. Without looking around, Edgar roared off into the distance, back to Paris.

As Edgar disappeared into the distance it started to rain. Duchess, who had been thrown out of the basket when it had landed on the bank of the river, stirred as she felt the raindrops fall heavily on her face. She stood up groggily, and shook her head, trying to remember where she was.

Suddenly there was a deafening clap of thunder, and an enormous dark cloud obscured the moon overhead. Fearing the worst, she looked anxiously for Marie, Toulouse and Berlioz.

"Children, where are you?" she cried. She found she had to shout now to make herself heard above the noise of the rain and the wind. "Where are you?"

"Here I am, Mama," came a tiny and frightened voice. Duchess looked up and sighed with relief. Marie was in the lower branches of a tree, where she had been thrown when the basket had landed on the ground.

Duchess scampered up the tree, and gently helped her daughter down to the ground. "Are you all right, Marie, darling?" Duchess asked anxiously.

Marie nodded. "I guess I had a nightmare and fell

out of bed," she said, and then her voice trailed off as she took in her new surroundings.

Apart from her one trip in Madame's carriage, Marie had never been outside the luxurious setting of Madame's mansion before; she was suddenly very scared indeed.

"Don't be frightened," her mother encouraged her, as they sheltered from the rain under the tree. Duchess's eyes darted this way and that as she tried to find Toulouse and Berlioz.

Suddenly, a bedraggled and very wet Berlioz emerged from the bushes. He had been flung into the water, and had awoken to find a curious frog staring at him. The sight had terrified him, and he ran to his mother, with the inquisitive frog hopping after him.

Duchess laughed fondly at her little son as he hid between her legs. The frog looked at him as though to say that he thought Berlioz was behaving like a very silly sort of cat, and then hopped away.

There was still no sign of Toulouse. In the storm Duchess realised that he wouldn't last long out in the open, and left Berlioz and Marie underneath the tree while she went off to look for him.

As she walked off, Berlioz and Marie peered into the basket which they had all forgotten about in the mud. There, still fast asleep, was their brother.

"Toulouse!" they both cried at once.

Toulouse woke up, rubbed the sleep out of his eyes,

and wondered why his brother and sister were looking down at him in such a curious manner. He also wondered what he was doing lying in a wicker basket, rather than the plush velvet cushions he was used to sleeping on in Madame's house.

"What's all this yelling about then?" he asked grumpily.

"Mama! He's been here all the time!" cried Marie.

Duchess ran back to the basket, and breathed a sigh of relief when she saw that her son was safe and sound.

"Are you all right?" she asked.

Toulouse frowned, unsure why he was being given all this special attention.

"I was having a funny dream," he said groggily. "Edgar was in it . . . and we were all riding and bouncing along . . ."

Just then the frog which had so frightened Berlioz returned, and let out an inquisitive croak.

"Frogs?" asked Toulouse and then was aware of the heavy rain drops splashing down on his face. His heart sank. "It wasn't a dream then?"

Three feline heads nodded as one.

Suddenly Toulouse sat bolt upright in his basket. "Edgar did this to us!" he said urgently.

"Edgar?" Duchess pooh-poohed the idea. "Why, that's ridiculous."

"Yeah," agreed Berlioz, who clearly thought that

the idea of the old butler cat-napping them was absurd. "Maybe you fell on your head, Toulouse?"

Toulouse shook his head, just as a mighty fork of lightning lit up the sky, followed a few seconds later by another enormous and deafening clap of thunder. They all looked up into the sky: the storm was getting worse by the minute.

"Mama, I'm afraid," whimpered Marie, and hid under her mother's body. "I want to go home . . ."

"Don't be frightened, darling," said Duchess, even though she was just as scared as her daughter. They had to find shelter from the night soon: otherwise they might all freeze to death; that is, if they didn't drown in the storm first!

Hurriedly she helped Marie and Berlioz into the basket to join Toulouse and then climbed in after them. She pulled the covering over the basket to afford them some protection from the pounding of the cold and heavy rain. Huddled together for warmth, they might just survive the night and the storm.

"What's going to happen to us?" asked Toulouse, trying hard to hide just how frightened he really was. Outside the noise of the storm was growing louder and louder.

"Darlings, I just don't know," admitted Duchess. She shivered and peeped out over the top of the basket. The rain was coming down in big heavy drops now. Already the ground was swimming in mud, and tree branches were rustling and crackling in the gale.

"It does look hopeless, doesn't it?" she said.

"I wish we were home with Madame right now," Berlioz dreamt aloud.

Duchess continued to peer out into the rain. "Poor Madame," she said, once again thinking not of herself but of another's happiness. "She'll be worried when she finds us gone . . ."

Back home in Paris, the storm was just as wild and violent as it was in the countryside. The lightning flashed in the sky, lighting up the whole of Paris from the Eiffel Tower to the great cathedral of Notre Dame. In her bedroom the noise of the crashing thunder, and the pounding of the raindrops on her window pane awoke Madame from a terrible nightmare.

She had had the most horrible dream. She had dreamt that Duchess and her three kittens had gone missing, and were lost somewhere out there in the storm.

She chided herself for being a silly old worrier, but, just to be sure, she got up out of her bed and walked over to the cats' bed at the foot of the window.

"Now, now, my darlings, don't be frightened," she said, "the storm will soon pass . . ."

Madame placed her hand underneath the cover of

the cat bed and frowned: there was nothing there! She ripped away the covers from the bed: it was empty.

"Oh no, they are gone!" she gasped as her nightmare suddenly became a horrible reality.

She turned on her heels and ran out of the bedroom door, down the corridor, crying the Aristocats' names. "They're gone! They're gone!" she cried as she woke up her entire household staff.

Roquefort had just left his mousehole, having been woken by all the commotion. He ran to the bedroom window and looked out at the pouring rain. Anything could happen to Duchess and her kittens on a night like this, he realised. They could get washed down a storm drain or even struck by lightning!

The tiny mouse came to a decision. Duchess and her three children had shown him many kindnesses over the past few years. Now it was his turn to repay the favour.

He ran back into his mousehole, and came back out a moment later, wearing his red raincoat and a deerstalker hat. Jumping down the steps two at a time he reached the ground floor of the mansion and raced out through the back door which had been left slightly ajar.

He ran out into the streets, calling out his friends' names.

"Duchess! Marie! Toulouse! Berlioz!"

But there was no reply, only the mighty and

30

implacable roar of the thunder and the sound of the rain as it pounded relentlessly down on the cobble-stoned streets of Paris. It seemed that Duchess and her three kittens were gone and lost forever.

4

Duchess was the first to wake up the following morning. The storm had faded and the ground, although still a little damp, was now warm and welcoming as the early-morning sun shone down on it.

Duchess basked luxuriantly in its warmth, and rolled over, smelling the dew and the flowers. Just a few minutes more, she told herself, before I wake the children.

She started as she heard the sound of someone singing, a little way off. Curious, she stood up and walked in the direction of the noise.

On the opposite bank of the river a large and handsome ginger tomcat was singing happily to himself. There was something curiously endearing about him, as he danced on the opposite bank, unaware of the fact that he was being watched.

His voice was brash and bawdy, unlike the refined and aristocatic accents of Duchess and her children.

He clearly belonged to the sort of class Madame would never have let Duchess associate with back in Paris; in short, he was a common alley cat!

Nevertheless, despite herself, Duchess couldn't help but watch, fascinated, as the alley cat danced on the bank, on the bridge over the stream, and then over to her side of the river. Unlike Duchess's own singing voice, his was loud and raucous but full of natural rhythm. As he continued singing about his life as an alley cat, Duchess even felt her paws tapping along with the music.

Still unaware of her presence, the alleycat climbed a tree, even managing to dance on one of the larger branches. As the branches shook, flowers fell off them, showering Duchess with their white and pink petals.

Down below Duchess laughed at his antics and at his song lyrics. In the song, he sang his name— Abraham Delacey, Giuseppe, Casey, Thomas O'Malley. "Why, monsieur," she chuckled. "Your name seems to cover all of Europe!"

Still in the branches of the tree, O'Malley turned and saw Duchess for the first time. And what he saw he liked very much indeed: Duchess was a very classy kind of cat, he decided. Without missing a beat, he plucked a flower from the tree and threw it down to Duchess, who caught it in her paws.

"Of course!" he said, and began to clamber down

33

the tree as if he had been doing it all his life (which, as a matter of fact, he had been doing). "I'm the only cat of my kind."

He landed on the ground and pranced over to Duchess, who sat there, coyly licking her paw.

By this time Marie, Toulouse and Berlioz had all woken up and were watching shyly from the rim of their basket. O'Malley was so taken with serenading Duchess that he didn't even notice them.

"Oh boy!" said Toulouse, scarcely able to believe his own good luck. "An alleycat!"

"Ssssh!" hissed Marie and clamped a paw over her brother's mouth. "Listen!"

O'Malley was now preening himself in front of their mother, who was watching him with a great deal of interest. He continued to sing about his wandering life as an alley cat.

Duchess could contain herself no longer and she clapped her paws together. "Bravo! Bravo!" she said, as though she might have been applauding someone at the Opera House in Paris. "You're very good! A great talent!"

O'Malley pretended not to care, but it was obvious that he was enjoying the praise—and from such a beautiful Aristocat as well. He sat down on a rock next to Duchess.

"And what might your name be?" he asked.

Duchess paused for a moment, a little disconcerted.

34

After all, in her social circles one was supposed to wait to be introduced. She wondered what Madame would say now if she knew that she was associating with a common and lowly alley cat!

Finally she said, a little too primly: "My name is Duchess."

O'Malley nodded appreciatively; he was right—this was one classy dame, that was for sure!

"Beautiful!" he said. "I love it!"

He stared into Duchess's face. "And those eyes! Whoooooo!" He shivered with delight, oblivious to the presence of the three kittens in the basket who were drinking in every word.

"Why, your eyes are like sapphires!" he claimed, and Duchess turned coyly away, while secretly smiling to herself. O'Malley continued: "They make the morning radiant and light!"

In the basket Marie sighed, "How romantic!"

Berlioz looked at his sister in disgust. "Sissy stuff!" he said dismissively.

Duchess, however, didn't consider O'Malley's compliments to be "sissy stuff" at all. She blushed slightly and smiled at O'Malley.

"*C'est tres jolie, monsieur,*" she said. "Very poetic!"

O'Malley grinned from ear to ear until Duchess added: "But it's not quite Shakespeare!"

"Of course not!" said O'Malley, not put out at all, as if he considered William Shakespeare to be a very inferior poet indeed. "That's pure O'Malley, baby! Right off the cuff!" He sniggered. "I got a million of 'em!"

He was about to deliver another of his much-used chat-up lines when Duchess raised a paw to stop him.

"No more, please," she begged, and then bowed her head. Now wasn't the time to be exchanging compliments with complete strangers. "I'm really in a great deal of trouble . . ."

O'Malley leapt off the rock on which he had been sitting, and flung himself at Duchess's feet.

"Trouble?" he asked. "Helping beautiful dames—" he corrected himself—"damsels in distress, is my specialty!" He looked up into Duchess's eyes. "Now, what's the hang-up, your Ladyship?"

Duchess wasn't quite sure what a "hang-up" was, but answered anyway.

"It is most important that I get back to Paris," she said, and glanced over at her three kittens whom O'Malley still hadn't noticed. "So if you would just be so kind and show me the way . . ."

"Show you the way?" asked O'Malley. "Perish the thought!"

He leapt to his feet and sidled up romantically against Duchess. "We shall fly to Paris on a magic carpet, side by side!" he declared.

Such promises were too much for little Marie to

bear. She leapt out of the basket and ran over to her mother's side.

"With the stars as our guide!" O'Malley continued. "Just we two!"

"That would be wonderful!" piped up Marie, and O'Malley looked down to see the little kitten's face beaming up at him. His face fell.

"*Three*?" he asked in disbelief.

Berlioz came over to him. O'Malley's face fell even further. "*Four*?"

Finally Toulouse joined them. O'Malley's face could fall no further so he just looked on in sheer horror. Would he never learn to keep his big mouth shut? What had he gone and let himself in for now? he asked himself.

"*Five*?"

Duchess smiled and nodded. "Yes, Monsieur O'Malley," she said, and indicated Marie, Berlioz and Toulouse. "These are my children."

"Oh, how sweet," said O'Malley in a voice which indicated that he clearly didn't mean it.

"Do you really have a magic carpet?" Berlioz asked him.

"And are we really going to ride on it?" asked Marie.

O'Malley wasn't quite sure what to say, but Marie didn't wait for an answer. She turned to Duchess. "Mama, do I have sparkling sapphire eyes that dazzle too?"

Duchess looked over at O'Malley who was sitting on the rock again. "Did I say that?" he groaned.

Duchess nodded. "Yes—right off your cuff," she said, repeating the alley cat's own words.

"And you also said that we're gonna ride on your magic carpet," Berlioz reminded him.

O'Malley was now clearly embarrassed. What had started off as nothing more than a chat-up line on his part was getting dangerously out of hand! "Well, now . . . er . . . what I meant, you see . . . I . . ."

"There is no poetry to cover this situation, is there, monsieur?" asked Duchess meaningfully.

O'Malley harrumphed. "Well, what I had in mind was a kind of a sports model, baby . . ." he said lamely. The three kittens looked at each other, uncomprehending, but Duchess understood what O'Malley was trying to say.

"Perhaps you meant a magic carpet built for two?" she asked.

Little Marie spoke up again. "I wouldn't take up too much room," she promised.

O'Malley stared awkwardly into space, until Duchess sighed. Men! she thought. They were all alike! All talk and no action! And alley cats were even worse!

"I understand perfectly, Monsieur O'Malley," she said, her voice suddenly full of disappointment. She turned to her children who looked at her with wide mournful eyes. "Come along . . ."

Marie sighed, and she and Berlioz slowly followed their mother as she moved off in what she supposed just might be the direction for Paris.

Toulouse stopped for a moment and raised his fists playfully at O'Malley. "I'm a tough alley cat too," he claimed and began to punch the air in front of him.

O'Malley grinned. "I bet you're a real tiger in your neighbourhood," he said, correctly guessing that Toulouse's "neighbourhood" didn't really extend much beyond Madame's front door.

"Yeah," said Toulouse, trying his hardest to sound like a real tough guy. "That's 'cos I practise all the time!"

"*Come along now, Toulouse!*" came Duchess's stern voice. Toulouse gave a helpless shrug and followed his mother and brother and sister.

"See you around, Tiger," smiled O'Malley, and waved as he watched the family leave.

"That's quite a family," O'Malley said to himself, and was suddenly filled with a sense of guilt. All Duchess and her family wanted was a little help to get home to Paris, and here he was, turning them down! What kind of cat was he after all? A sucker for a hard-luck story, that's what!

"You're not a cat, O'Malley!" he told himself

angrily. "You're a rat!" He started to run after Duchess and the others. "Hey! Hold up there!"

They stopped and turned to look at him. "Yes, Monsieur O'Malley?" asked Duchess.

O'Malley leant down and looked at the three kittens. They looked up at him with expectant and hopeful eyes.

"Now look, kids," he said. "If I said a magic carpet then a magic carpet it's gonna be!"

Marie, Berlioz and Toulouse looked wonderingly at each other: they could hardly believe their luck.

O'Malley continued: "And it's gonna stop for passengers! And it's gonna stop right here!"

Marie, Berlioz and Toulouse all let out a cheer of joy. "Oh, boy, we're all gonna fly after all!" shouted Berlioz.

Duchess considered O'Malley warily. "Is this another flight of fantasy, Monsieur O'Malley?" she asked.

O'Malley grinned. "No, no, no, baby!" he insisted.

If Duchess and the kids were going to get home to Paris then Abraham Delacey Giuseppe Casey Thomas O'Malley the Alley Cat was just the cat who was going to do it!

5

"Now you all just hide over there," said O'Malley as he hurried Duchess and her kittens behind the cover of a clump of bushes, by the side of the road which, he told them, led to Paris. They all did as he said.

"Now you just leave the rest to Thomas O'Malley," said the alley cat, and Duchess looked quizzically at him. What great plan did O'Malley have in store for them?

When Duchess and her kittens were safely hidden behind the bushes, O'Malley climbed up a large tree which stood by the side of the road, and positioned himself on one of the branches which hung over the road. Now all he needed, he told the kittens, was a magic carpet!

It wasn't long in coming. They had been in hiding for only a few minutes when a small van appeared on the horizon.

"One magic carpet coming up!" announced

O'Malley.

"That's a magic carpet?" asked Duchess, with a mixture of amusement and disbelief. O'Malley might call the tiny vehicle which was coming down the road, a magic carpet; she, however, recognised it as a milk van, one of many which daily carried barrels of milk from the country farms to Paris.

O'Malley nodded happily and waited. As soon as the milk van was directly underneath him, he dropped from the overhanging branch and landed with a *thunk*! on the van's bonnet.

He climbed up on the van's windscreen, until he could see the driver's face. Then he bared his teeth and let out a blood-curling howl.

The driver, terrified out of his wits by the sudden appearance of a mad cat, yelped with terror, and veered off the road. O'Malley continued to pull faces at the frightened man as he came to an unsteady halt, just by the bush where Duchess and her kittens were waiting in hiding.

The milkman jumped out of the driver's seat and shook his fist at O'Malley, who leapt off the bonnet and disappeared into the bushes.

"Stupid cat!" he cried angrily, as he walked to the front of his van to crank up the engine again. "Brainless lunatic!"

Ignoring the milkman's curses, O'Malley quickly ushered Duchess and her family out of the bushes

Above: Madame Adelaide strokes Duchess, her graceful white
pedigree cat.

Below: Edgar has just heard that Madame Adelaide is leaving
him her vast fortune – after her cats have died.

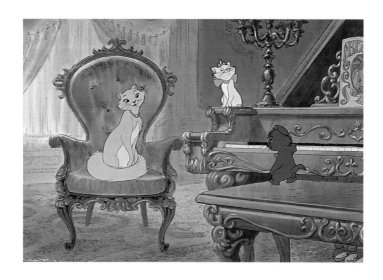

Above: Duchess teaches her kittens that they must grow up to be real Aristocats and they learn their scales and arpeggios.

Below: Edgar concocts a sleeping potion which he will feed to the Aristocats – he is determined to get rid of them.

Above: Duchess and the kittens have been catnapped by
Edgar, and wake up in the middle of nowhere.

Below: On the opposite bank of the river stands a large ginger
tom-cat – Thomas O'Malley, the alley cat.

Above: The kittens lap milk from a churn as they travel in the back of a milk van to Paris.

Below: Thomas, Duchess and the kittens hide underneath a train track as a train thunders past.

Above: Back in Paris, Abigail and Amelia, the English geese, meet up with their Uncle Waldo.

Below: Edgar attempts to get his belongings back from Napoleon and Lafayette.

Above: Thomas O'Malley is reunited with his old friend Scat Cat.

Below: Scat Cat and the rest of the Alley Cats play their wild jazz music.

Above: Duchess plays the harp while Thomas listens.

Below: Thomas and Duchess sit on the rooftops, their tails entwined, and talk about the future.

Above: Edgar has re-captured the Aristocats and is about to send them to Timbuktu.

Below: Thomas, Duchess and the kittens pose for a photograph at Madame Adelaide's house.

and onto the tailgate at the back of the van.

"Step lively there!" he said, keeping half an eye open for the milkman's return. "All aboard for Paris!"

When her three kittens were safely on board, Duchess turned to the alley cat, who was still standing in the middle of the road.

"Mister O'Malley, you could have lost your life there," she said, before joining the kittens on the tailgate.

O'Malley shrugged, as if stopping milk vans was something he did every day. "So, I've got a few to spare," he said. "It was nothin'."

"How can we ever thank you?" Duchess asked. Up front the milkman had returned to the driver's seat, unaware that he had some new passengers, and was revving up the engine, ready to move off again.

"My pleasure entirely," said O'Malley as he waved to the departing Duchess and her kittens. "Aloha! Auf wiedersehen, bon soir, sayonara—and all those goodbye things, baby!"

All four of the Aristocats waved goodbye to O'Malley as the milk van moved further and further away down the road in the direction of Paris. So fervently did Marie wave that she lost her balance and fell off the tailboard and into the road.

"Mama!" she screamed, and turned to see the milk van speed away.

O'Malley didn't even stop to think for one moment. Instead, he raced towards Marie, and picked her up gently in his mouth and ran with her towards the rapidly disappearing van.

Summoning up his very last reserves of strength he caught up with the van and leapt onto the tailgate, just managing to catch hold of it with his paws. He released Marie from his mouth and she scambled back to her mother. Meanwhile Duchess, Berlioz and Toulouse helped O'Malley onto the tailgate.

"Haven't we met someplace before?" O'Malley joked as Duchess pulled him aboard.

Duchess nodded and smiled. "And I'm so very glad we did!" she said.

Marie came up to O'Malley. "Thank you, Mister O'Malley, for saving my life," she said politely, just as well brought up Aristocats had been taught to do.

"Hey, no trouble at all, sweetheart," said O'Malley nonchalantly. He smiled: it seemed that he was fated to stick together with Duchess and her family for quite a while to come. "And when we get to Paris I'll show you all the time of your lives!"

Marie, Berlioz and Toulouse all cheered, until Duchess stepped forward.

"I'm so sorry, but we just couldn't . . ." she began. "You see, my mistress will be so worried about us . . ."

O'Malley sniffed, as if to say that he really didn't have much faith in human beings. "Humans don't really worry too much about their pets," he said off-handedly.

Duchess looked wistfully off into the distance. "You don't understand," she said. "She loves us very, very much. We can't leave her in that big mansion all alone . . . She always said that we were the greatest treasure she could ever own—because with us she never felt alone . . ."

The milk van rumbled on its way towards Paris.

Back in Paris, not only poor Madame, but also Roquefort and Frou-Frou, the mare, were feeling all alone. When Roquefort entered the stable, still dressed in the raincoat and deer-stalker he had been wearing last night, Frou-Frou trotted anxiously up to him.

"I've been so worried about you, Roquefort," she said. "Did you have any luck at all?"

Roquefort shook his head miserably. He had spent the whole night trying to track down Duchess and the kittens and hadn't been able to find a single clue.

"Poor Madame didn't get a wink of sleep," said Frou-Frou. Indeed the light from Madame Adelaide's window had blazed all night as she sent her servants to all corners of the city looking for her beloved Aristocats.

"It's such a sad day for all of us," complained Roquefort.

Just at that moment Edgar entered the stable carrying a pail of water and a rolled-up newspaper. Frou-Frou and Roquefort exchanged worried looks. Of all the people in Madame's household, Edgar had been the only one who hadn't been distressed by the kittens' disappearance: indeed as he entered the stable he was whistling a happy tune to himself.

"Good morning, Frou-Frou, my pretty steed," he said, as he put down the pail and patted the mare on the nose. He held up the newspaper so she could see it. "I've some news here straight from the horse's mouth—"he giggled—"If you'll pardon the expression of course!"

Frou-Frou looked curiously at Edgar as the butler continued. "Look, Frou-Frou," he boasted, "I've made the headlines!"

He opened the newspaper at the front page and read the headline out loud. "'Mysterious cat-napper abducts family of cats'!" He laughed. "Aren't you proud of me!"

"So *he's* the catnapper!" Roquefort finally realised. He'd suspected Edgar ever since the sleeping pills in the kittens' late-night bowl of hot milk: now here was definite proof!

Edgar chortled with glee. "The police said it was a professional, masterful job," he said. "The work of a genius! Not bad, eh, Frou-Frou, old girl?"

Frou-Frou whinnied, as if to tell Edgar exactly what she thought of him.

"And they won't find a single clue to implicate me," he continued as he started to leave the stable. Then he suddenly stopped. His face went as white as a sheet.

"My hat! My umbrella," he cried nervously, as he remembered he had left them behind in the fight with Napoleon and Lafayette. If the police found them, they could be used as evidence against him. "I've got to get those things back tonight!" he determined. Edgar stalked out of the stable. Suddenly he was a very worried man indeed.

Roquefort and Frou-Frou watched him go. "That sneaky, crooked, no-good butler!" hissed Roquefort.

6

The journey to Paris was not without its problems. As the milk van bumped along over the uneven back roads leading to the French capital, the kittens' stomachs began to rumble. It had been a long time since they had last eaten, and they were all very hungry.

O'Malley led them to the corner of the milk van where he whipped a sack off a huge canister of cream. Duchess and her children all greedily lapped up the thick cream, making a great deal of noise. It was then that the driver of the milk van saw them in his rear-view mirror.

"Thieves! Robbers!" he cried.

O'Malley didn't waste a second. He leapt on the driver's head, forcing him to stop the truck. As the driver struggled to free himself from the alley cat, Duchess and her kittens took advantage of O'Malley's diversion to leap out of the back of the van.

As soon as Duchess and the kittens were safely out

of danger, O'Malley jumped off the driver's head and raced to join them.

The enraged driver leapt out of his seat and ran after them, screaming and cursing.

"Mangy tramps! Take that!" he cried, as he threw a wrench after the fleeing cats. It narrowly missed Duchess and she yelped in panic. Berlioz and Toulouse, however, seemed to be enjoying the chase immensely.

The driver grabbed an empty bucket from the back of his van and threw it at Marie. It almost struck her but, in the very nick of time, O'Malley grabbed the little kitten in his mouth and ran after Duchess and the others towards the railway tracks which ran parallel to the road.

There they managed to find shelter behind a tool shed, out of sight of the angry milkman, who soon gave up his search for them and returned to his van.

Duchess peeped out from behind the tool shed and breathed a sigh of relief as she watched the milk van rumble away off into the distance.

"What a horrible human!" she said.

O'Malley sighed. "Some humans are like that, Duchess," he said. It was obvious that Duchess and the kittens, with their fine and sheltered upbringing, had never come into contact with such people before. "I've learnt to live with them . . ."

Satisfied that they were now in no more danger,

Toulouse came out of hiding and shook his tiny fists at the departing milk van.

"I'll show him!" he said, and began to run after the van, until O'Malley called him back.

"Hey, cool it, li'l tiger," he said, and chuckled at the kitten's feistiness. "That guy's dynamite!"

"But he called us tramps!" protested Toulouse.

Duchess hushed her son. "I'll be so glad when we get back home," she said wistfully. The comfortable velvet cushions and fine food and warm milk of Madame's mansion still seemed just as far away as ever.

"That's still a long way off," said O'Malley, and added practically: "so we'd better get moving!"

By the middle of the afternoon the cats were exhausted and weary. They had spent most of the day following the railway track which, O'Malley had reassured them, led straight to Paris.

Part of the railway crossed over a bridge, beneath which flowed a river. As the cats marched across the bridge in single file, they heard a whistle and then a thundering noise behind them. A train was approaching them at full speed!

Duchess and her kittens stood transfixed, like rabbits caught in the glare of a car's headlights, as the train rumbled towards them.

"Don't panic!" cried O'Malley. "Down here!" He

slunk between the slats of the railway tracks to one of the supporting trestles underneath. The others followed him, and they stayed there until the train had passed overhead. As the noise of the train disappeared they all heard a frightened little voice.

"Mama! Mama!"

Duchess quickly looked around her. Marie! Where was Marie?

Down below them in the water Marie was struggling to stay afloat. In all the excitement no one had heard the kitten fall into the river.

"Keep your head up, Marie!" called out O'Malley. "Here I come!".

The alley cat leapt off the bridge and with a tremendous *splash*! landed in the water only a few feet away from Marie. There wasn't a second to lose: the current in this part of the river was strong, and within seconds it would carry her away from them forever! Up above, Duchess and her sons watched on anxiously as O'Malley swam over to Marie.

Fighting against the current, O'Malley managed to reach Marie and grabbed her with his mouth. A log was floating close by, and, with powerful strokes, O'Malley swam over to it. The current was dragging them along but, with difficulty, he managed to put Marie onto the log.

Meanwhile, Duchess and the boys had come down from the bridge and were running along the river

51

bank. A tree was growing on the side of the bank and Duchess climbed onto one of the branches which reached over the river.

The current was quickly dragging Marie and O'Malley towards them now. Duchess knew she would have only one chance to rescue Marie.

As the log approached, she leant out as much as she dared from the overhanging branch.

O'Malley was still in the water, holding on to the log. As he and Marie approached the overhanging tree, he managed to lift Marie up into the waiting mouth of her mother. Duchess almost dropped her, but managed to drag her little girl to safety and back to the bank.

Toulouse and Berlioz ran up to join their sister. "Gee, Marie," said Toulouse, trying to conceal his relief at his sister's rescue. "Why did you have to fall off the bridge?"

Marie gave her brother the only reply his question deserved: she stuck her tongue out at him.

Duchess rushed back down to the river bank. "Thomas!" she cried. "Take care!"

O'Malley had finally climbed onto the floating log which was being rapidly carried along by the current. He waved cheerfully at the Aristocats as he rushed past them.

"I'm all right, honey!" he called out to Duchess.

"Don't worry about me—I'll see you all downstream!"

A little way downstream two geese were out for an early-afternoon stroll along the river bank. Tall and proud, they walked with their beaks held high in the air, and wore dainty and expensive pink and blue bonnets on their heads. They seemed every inch ladies.

"What beautiful countryside, Abigail," one of the geese said to her companion, as she admired the rolling French hills, and the river which sparkled blue and silver in the sunlight. "So much like our own dear England."

"Indeed," said her companion, whose voice was just as posh and upper-class as her friend's. She looked longingly at the river's inviting water. "Amelia, if I walk much further I'll get flat feet."

"Abigail," Amelia pointed out, "we were born with flat feet!"

She honked with laughter: sometimes Abigail did come out with the most absurd comments!

Abigail laughed too and then, with an outstretched wing, pointed at the figure of O'Malley as he floated down the river on the log. They watched in amazement as he jumped into the water and grabbed hold of an overhanging willow branch with his mouth, and tried to pull himself to shore.

"Fancy that!" said Abigail, as she and Amelia

walked down to the river's edge. "A cat learning to swim!"

"And he's going about it all the wrong way," said Amelia. She splashed into the water and started swimming towards the alley cat.

"Quite," agreed Abigail snootily. "And we must correct him!"

They sailed towards O'Malley who was now struggling in the water. Cats weren't supposed to like swimming, he knew, and now he realised why. The river was wet, deep, and very, very cold.

Amelia and Abigail circled O'Malley.

"You are most fortunate that we happened along, sir," said Amelia.

"We're here to help you," added Abigail.

O'Malley, who still had the willow branch in his mouth and was trying to pull himself up onto the river bank, tried to shoo them away.

"Back off, girls," he said, releasing his hold of the branch. The current began to sweep him away, and he snatched at the branch again.

Abigail, who obviously thought that O'Malley was trying to learn how to swim, rather than save himself from drowning, sniffed.

"First you must gain self-confidence by striking out on your own," she said, sounding exactly like a rather haughty schoolteacher.

Amelia sighed. "You will never learn to swim with

that willow branch in your mouth," she remarked.

O'Malley by now had almost reached the river bank and was about to haul himself onto the rocks, when the two well-meaning geese started to snip away at the branch with their beaks.

"Don't do that!" yelped O'Malley, but it was too late. The geese had cut the willow branch, separating it from the tree, and the current swept O'Malley away. He sank under the water, as the geese moved towards him, totally unconcerned at his predicament.

"You're doing splendidly," Abigail encouraged him.

O'Malley came to the surface and floundered about in the water before sinking again.

"And don't worry about form," said Amelia. "That will come later!"

O'Malley surfaced and then went under for the third and final time.

"He takes to water like a fish, doesn't he?" said Abigail.

Suddenly Amelia felt someone grab her tail-feathers. Thinking that the drowning alley cat was wanting to play a game of underwater tag, she laughed and swam away.

"Now this is no time for fun and games!" she chortled.

There was no reply, and no sign of O'Malley either. Abigail and Amelia exchanged anxious looks.

"Gracious, Amelia," said a worried Abigail. "You don't suppose . . ."

Amelia nodded guiltily. "Yes, I do," she sighed. "Well, bottoms up!"

The two geese dived underwater in search of O'Malley.

7

Duchess and the kittens finally caught up with O'Malley as he was being helped out of the water by Amelia and Abigail. Both of the geese were clucking their apologies as O'Malley stood in the shallows. He was wet and bedraggled, and obviously wasn't going to forgive the two geese in a hurry.

Duchess rushed up to O'Malley. "Thomas! Thank goodness you're safe!" she said gratefully and hugged him.

Toulouse splashed in the water to O'Malley's side. "Can I help you, Mister O'Malley?" he asked.

O'Malley glared at Amelia and Abigail who were now standing a little way off. "Help?" he growled. "I've had all the help I can take!"

"You really did quite well for a beginner . . ." Abigail pointed out kindly.

Duchess came up to the two geese. "Thank you so much for helping Mister O'Malley," she said.

The geese nodded, delighted to have at last found

someone with the good manners and breeding to say "thank you".

Amelia urged Duchess not to mention it and introduced herself and Abigail to the Aristocats.

Berlioz pointed down to the geeses' feet. "Look, they've got rubber feet!" he said. Duchess tried to hush him, but Amelia and Abigail just giggled.

"We're on a walking tour of France," explained Amelia.

"Swimming some of the way of course," added Abigail.

Duchess led the geese back to the river bank where O'Malley was shaking himself dry, and introduced the two geese to him.

"Get those two web-footed lifeguards outta here!" he said.

"Now, now, Thomas," Duchess chided, resolving that sooner or later she would have to teach this rough and ready alley cat some manners. (And she discovered that she was rather looking forward to the prospect too . . .)

O'Malley wrung out his tail, and shrugged. He supposed that these two geese had saved his life after all—even though it was they who very nearly drowned him in the first place!

"Hiya, chicks!" he said casually. The geese laughed.

"We're not chickens," said Abigail, "we're geese!"

58

O'Malley grinned and there was a sly look in his eyes. "I thought you were swans!"

The geese burst into giggles again as O'Malley worked his much-used charms on them.

"Flatterer!" said Amelia.

Abigail turned to Duchess who had just shot an angry look at O'Malley.

"Your husband is very charming," she said. "And very handsome."

O'Malley laughed. "Ah . . . well, I'm not exactly her husband . . ." he admitted.

"Not exactly?" asked Amelia, a little primly. "You either are or you're not!"

"All right, I'm not."

Amelia and Abigail looked shocked: they obviously thought the worst.

"It's scandalous!" said Amelia.

"He's nothing but a cad!" agreed Abigail, forgetting that only seconds ago she had been singing O'Malley's praises.

"He's obviously a philanderer," snorted Amelia. "One who trifles with unsuspecting women's hearts!"

Duchess hurried to try and clear up the misunderstanding. "Thomas is a dear friend of ours, who's just helping us to get to . . ."

"Come on, Duchess," urged O'Malley, who had had enough of the geese casting doubts on his character. "Let's get outta here." He waved Amelia and Abigail goodbye. "See you around, girls! We're on our way to Paris."

"We're going to Paris ourselves," said Abigail.

O'Malley groaned: he could see what was going to come next!

"Why don't you join us?" asked Amelia.

"I think that's a splendid idea!" said Duchess, before O'Malley had a chance to say no.

The two geese clucked happily and began to arrange Duchess and the kittens in a "v" formation. Reluctantly O'Malley agreed to bring up the rear.

Abigail examined the Aristocats like a general surveying her troops. Satisfied that everyone was where they should be, she shouted "Forward—march!" and led the way ahead.

"Mama," asked Berlioz, as he followed the two geese, "do we have to waddle like they do?"

"Yes, dear," chuckled Duchess, "think goose!"

So, with their bottoms all waving this way and that, the two geese, four Aristocats, and one extremely disgruntled alley cat, all waddled off on the road to Paris.

8

L ate at night, the Aristocats finally reached the
outskirts of Paris where they said goodbye to
Amelia and Abigail. Now they were walking along the
high Parisian rooftops, taking in the sights and sounds
of the city they thought they would never see again. In
the distance the great bells of Notre Dame Cathedral
tolled the half-hour; they could just see the Eiffel
Tower at the far end of town, silhouetted in the
moonlight.

Marie, who was riding on O'Malley's back,
yawned. It was very late—in fact, she had never
stayed up this late before in her life. After all the
action of the past day she was very tired, and even
Berlioz and Toulouse dreamt of sleeping on their own
velvet cushions back at Madame's mansion.

"Thomas, Madame will be so worried," said
Duchess. "Are you sure we can't get home tonight?"

"Look, baby, it's late," he reminded her. "The kids
are bushed."

Toulouse agreed. "I bet we walked a hundred miles," he yawned.

"I'll bet it's more like a thousand," Berlioz said gloomily. His feet were hurting him, and all he really wanted to do right now was lie down and sleep. He would be quite happy to do it on the rooftop, if only his mother would let him. Sleeping like an alley cat for one night might even be fun, he decided.

"Cheer up, darlings," said Duchess. "Mister O'Malley knows of a place where we can stay tonight." She sounded a little doubtful, wondering what sort of places a common alley cat might frequent.

"How much further is it, Mister O'Malley?" asked Toulouse, and yawned again.

"Keep your whiskers up, tiger," he said cheerfully. "It's just behind that next chimney."

By the next chimney there was a broken skylight which looked down into a large run-down old attic.

"There it is," said O'Malley, "my very own penthouse flat!" He noticed the look of disappointment on Duchess's face. "I know it's not exactly the Ritz, but . . ."

Marie had jumped off O'Malley's back and had run over to her brothers who were peering down through the skylight into the attic.

"It's peaceful and quiet, and you'll be able to . . ."

The noise of loud and rowdy jazz music suddenly

blasted up from out of the attic, and O'Malley's face broke into a smile.

"Uh-oh, it sounds like Scat Cat and his gang have dropped by," he said. Something told him that this night wasn't going to be as peaceful and as quiet as he had promised Duchess.

As her kittens' eyes lit up, Duchess asked O'Malley who Scat Cat and his gang were. "Are they friends of yours?"

"Yeah," said O'Malley. "They're old buddies— and they're real swingers!"

"Swingers?" asked Duchess. "What is a swinger?"

O'Malley tried to think of a way to describe his friends to this well brought up feline. Finally he said, rather lamely: "They're not exactly your type, Duchess . . . Maybe we'd better find another place?"

Duchess shook her head. She had always been told to be polite and show an interest in other people's lives and friends. Besides, she discovered that she was liking this resourceful and rough and ready alley cat more and more.

"No, I would like to see your pad," she said, wondering what she was letting herself in for, "and meet your 'Scat Cat'."

He and Duchess joined the kittens at the skylight, and as O'Malley peered down into the attic he shouted down: "Hey, Scat Cat! Blow some of that sweet music my way!"

Down in the attic a big, fat cat wearing a pork pie hat was lying on a ramshackle bed. He grinned when he saw O'Malley's face.

"Well, lookie here!" he whooped. "Big man O'Malley is back in his alley! Swing down here, Daddy!"

O'Malley came down with the others into the attic and shook paws with Scat Cat. There were other cats in the attic too, all of them playing wild and bouncy music.

An English cat, who was playing a guitar, and wearing hippy glasses and a bandana said: "Welcome home, O'Malley," in a trendy London accent; while a fat Italian cat playing a squeeze box wished O'Malley a "buona sera".

O'Malley introduced the kittens and Duchess to Scat Cat. Scat Cat kissed Duchess extravagantly on the paw.

Duchess listened to the jazz music that the other cats were playing. Up to now, the only music Duchess had ever heard had been the classical pieces Madame had played on the piano, or arias from the great operas she had sung in. This new music was so different, so joyous, so *alive*. Already her paws were tapping in time to the rhythm.

"It isn't Beethoven, Mama," said Berlioz, who had joined another cat at a broken-down piano, "but it sure bounces!"

Scat Cat chuckled. "Say, this kitten-cat sure knows where it's at!"

"Knows where what's at?" asked Marie, who had found a seat for herself on an overturned clothes trunk.

She wasn't sure that a young lady like herself should be in a place like this, but nevertheless was enjoying herself immensely.

"Well, little lady, let me elucidate here!" said Scat Cat, and clicked a finger at his friends. They all knew that this was a signal for their boss to get on down to his favourite song.

Scat Cat sang about how *everyone* really wants to be a cat, and behind him his musicians grooved into the catchy beat.

O'Malley was getting into the swing of things now and joined Scat Cat: cats really do have rhythm and style!

By now everyone was joining in and the whole joint was jumping. Marie, Toulouse and Berlioz were swinging to the wild music that Scat Cat and his friends were playing. Even O'Malley and Duchess were dancing together, having the time of their lives.

Duchess had never ever behaved like this in her life, but there was something in this new music that set her paws a-tapping and her heart a-leaping like never before. She was enjoying herself immensely, dancing with O'Malley, in this room full of the sort of cats she would never have met if she had stayed forever in Madame's house.

Yes, it was good to be alive, decided Duchess, dancing to jazz in Paris with O'Malley. It was great to be a cat, an Aristocat, an alley cat, why, any sort of cat in fact—because, like the song said, a cat's the only cat that knows where it's at!

After the party had ended Duchess put her three kittens to sleep in O'Malley's bed and then climbed on the roof to join the alley cat. They looked over the roof tops of Paris: the city looked beautiful in the moonlight.

"Thomas, your friends are really delightful," said Duchess. This time, she wasn't just being polite; she really meant it.

"They're kind of rough around the edges," he admitted. "But if you're ever in a jam, they're right there."

"And when we needed *you*, you were right there too," said Duchess.

O'Malley shrugged, for once at a loss for words. Finally he said: "That was just a lucky break—for *me*, baby." He laughed awkwardly. "Gee, that's pretty corny, isn't it?"

Duchess smiled. "No, not at all. Any woman would like it . . . even little Marie."

In fact little Marie was closer than either Duchess

or O'Malley had realised. She, Toulouse and Berlioz had woken up and climbed up to the roof to eavesdrop on their mother and O'Malley.

She swooned as O'Malley tried to express his feelings towards her mother; as she did, Berlioz, like a typical boy, stuck his tongue out at her.

"I love those little kittens," O'Malley said to Duchess.

"And they are very fond of you too," said Duchess. Unseen by her or O'Malley, Marie and Berlioz silently nodded their heads in agreement.

O'Malley and Duchess continued to look out over the rooftops of Paris. O'Malley curled his tail around Duchess's.

"They need a . . . a . . ." he began.

Duchess turned to look at him curiously. Was he going to say what she hoped he would?

"Well, you know . . . they need a sort of . . . of . . . well, a father around . . ."

Marie and Berlioz almost whooped for joy. Was O'Malley going to become their father?

Duchess smiled. "Thomas, that would be wonderful!" She paused for a minute, hoping a thousand different things, and then said: "And thank you so much for offering us your home . . . I mean, your pad. It's very nice."

"Wait a minute," said O'Malley. "This is the low-rent district, remember?"

"All it needs is a little tidying up," she protested. "A little feminine touch . . ."

Their eyes met; and there was now little need for words.

"Well, if you're applying for the job . . ." O'Malley said, trying to sound casual although in fact his heart was beating as fast as Duchess's.

Duchess sighed and turned away. "Oh, darling, if only I could . . ."

"But why can't you?" he asked. There was a note of panic in his voice.

"Because of Madame," Duchess reminded him. "I could never leave her."

O'Malley frowned: he couldn't understand Duchess's fondness for her mistress. "But Madame's just another human," he said. 'You're just her house pets!"

"No, no. We mean far more to her than that . . ." Duchess shook her head sadly. "I'm sorry, but we just have to go home tomorrow . . ."

Another long and awkward silence followed, until O'Malley said: "Well, I guess you know best . . . But I'm gonna miss you, baby, and those kids."

Unheard by either Duchess or O'Malley the three kittens sighed.

"Well," said Berlioz, "we almost had a father . . ."

"Yeah," said Toulouse sadly. "C'mon, let's go back to bed."

68

So the three kittens left Duchess and O'Malley to watch the sun rise over Paris in silence.

In their heart of hearts the two cats knew that they belonged together. But what could an Aristocat and an alley cat possibly have in common?

9

It was Roquefort who saw them first. He had been sitting by the window, watching the sun come up over Paris when he saw the big ginger alley cat turn the corner and walk, bold as brass, up the drive to Madame Adelaide's house.

And following right behind him, their tails held high in the air, were Duchess and her three kittens!

He let out a squeak of excitement and slid down the curtain, heading for the front door to welcome the Aristocats back. Suddenly he remembered Edgar. Edgar had spent most of the night fishing in the river to retrieve his hat and umbrella. Now he had returned. If the crafty old butler discovered that Duchess and her kittens had escaped . . .

Roquefort ran to the pantry where the butler was drinking champagne and congratulating himself on his evil deeds. As he dreamt of all the things he could buy with Madame's riches, Roquefort tied his shoelaces together . . .

Outside, overjoyed to be back home once more, Marie, Toulouse and Berlioz bounded up to the front door of Madame's mansion. They frowned when they saw that the cat flap which they usually used to get in and out of the grand house was locked. They looked at each other, unsure of what to do next.

"Let's start meowing," suggested Marie, and they all began to meow at the top of their voices, hoping to attract Madame Adelaide's attention.

However, Madame was getting a little hard of hearing by now, and was unaware of the return of her beloved Aristocats. But down in the pantry, Edgar's face turned deathly pale.

"It can't be them!" he hissed, and stood up and ran for the stairs. He crashed to the floor as he tripped over the shoelaces that Roquefort had tied together.

Taking advantage of the slight delay, the little mouse leapt up the stairs two at a time and made for the front door.

In the street outside, Duchess and O'Malley were saying their final goodbyes. It was a painful and tearful parting for both of them. In the short time they had been together, they had come to rely on and respect each other. They were going to miss each other dreadfully.

"I don't know what to say," said Duchess sadly. "I only wish that . . ."

O'Malley smiled kindly, although deep inside he

was hurting as much as Duchess. "Maybe just a short sweet goodbye would be the easiest," he suggested.

There were tears in Duchess's eyes now. "I'll never forget you, Thomas O'Malley," she said.

"So long, baby," O'Malley said and slowly walked away down the road. Duchess sadly watched him go, and then turned to her children.

The kittens were all gazing up at Roquefort who had climbed back up the curtain and was standing at the window, waving and shouting at them. He was trying to warn them about Edgar, but the window-glass was too thick and they couldn't hear him.

"Hi, Roquefort!" they shouted cheerily.

"He's sure glad to see us," said Berlioz.

The front door opened, and Duchess and her kittens entered the mansion.

Edgar was peering down at them; in his hands he had a big sack.

"Why, Duchess, wherever have you been?" asked the cunning old butler.

In a flash he put the sack over Duchess and her kittens, scooping them up, and tying the mouth of the sack. Inside Duchess and her kittens squealed and struggled but it was no use: Edgar had them all in his power again!

"You came back!" he growled as he tied the knot even tighter. "That isn't fair!"

Suddenly, he heard Madame's voice coming from

upstairs, calling for him. Cursing, he shoved the sack into the oven, slamming the door behind it, and ran upstairs to see what his mistress wanted.

As soon as he had gone Roquefort ran over to the oven. He was too tiny and too weak to open the oven door, but he could hear the cats' cries as they shouted to him.

He put his ear to the door. "His name is *what*?" he asked, and concentrated as Duchess shouted back to him: "His name is O'Malley!"

"Abraham Delacey Giuseppe Casey . . ." added Marie helpfully.

Roquefort shook his head and ran off to the front door. All he knew was that there was only one creature in the world who could save Duchess and the kittens now—and that creature was heading off back to his own home, and out of Duchess's life for good!

Roquefort raced out of the mansion and out into the street. He looked this way and that, but there was no sign of O'Malley. Finally he caught sight of the ginger tom as he was about to turn the corner of the street. He ran as fast as his tiny legs would carry him.

"Mister O'Malley!" he cried, but the alley cat didn't hear him and continued walking despondently away. Summoning up his last reserves of strength, Roquefort ran even faster.

"Hey! Stop!" he screeched.

O'Malley turned, and seemed amazed to see a

73

mouse chasing after him. After all, it was supposed to be the other way round, he told himself; alley cats were supposed to chase mice!

Roquefort ran up to him, out of breath. "Duchess . . . kittens . . ." he panted. "In trouble! . . . The butler did it!"

O'Malley looked at the tiny mouse and then back at Madame's mansion. If anyone was threatening Duchess and the kittens then he had to stop them.

"You go get Scat Cat and his gang of alley cats!" he told Roquefort.

The mouse looked worried. "A . . . alley cats?" he stammered. "But I'm a mouse!" Somehow he didn't think that a band of mangy alley cats would be as tolerant of him as the refined Duchess and her kittens were.

"Look, I'm gonna need help!" O'Malley said firmly. "Just move!"

Deciding that his personal safety was nothing compared with the welfare of the Aristocats, Roquefort ran off down the road after O'Malley had told him where to find Scat Cat and the others.

"Tell 'em O'Malley sent you!" the alley cat called after him. "And you won't have a bit of trouble!"

"Huh! No trouble, he says," thought Roquefort as he raced through the dirty and dingy streets of Paris. "That's easy for . . . for what's his name to say . . ."

Roquefort had already forgotten O'Malley's name. "He's got nine lives. I've only got one!"

As he passed down a darkened alley, an enormous claw suddenly appeared from behind a garbage can. It grabbed Roquefort by the tail, and scooped him up into the air. The tiny mouse froze as he found himself staring into the mean face of a fierce-looking cat who dangled him in front of his greedy and hungry jaws.

"Well, well, well, what's a little swinger like you doin' on our side of town?" asked Scat Cat and licked his lips.

"I . . . I was sent here for help," said Roquefort as from behind the garbage can several other members of Scat's gang appeared. "I was sent here for help—by a cat!"

All the members of the gang burst out laughing. They had never heard such an outrageous and crazy story before. Scat dropped Roquefort and he rushed away, straight into the mouth of an upturned bottle. Another cat picked the bottle up and shook it, tipping Roquefort out into the waiting claws of one of his cronies.

"H . . . honest!" stammered the now terrified Roquefort. "He just told me to mention his name . . ."

"So start mentioning the name, rodent!" hissed one of the cats, who spoke with distinctive Russian accent.

"Hey, now don't rush me!" said Roquefort,

desperately playing for time. In truth, he couldn't remember the name of the ginger tom who had sent him on his mission. He thought hard. "O'Brien?" he said hopefully.

The cats all shook their heads.

"You do all believe me, don't you?" Roquefort spluttered. It was obvious that they didn't.

"Keep talkin', Mousey," said the English cat in the hippie shades.

"How about . . . O'Grady?"

Scat sighed. "I'm afraid you just struck out, Mousey," he said. He licked his lips once more and tickled Roquefort under the chin with a razor-sharp nail. "Any last requests?"

Roquefort gulped: it looked like the end. "Oh why did I ever listen to that O'Malley cat?" he despaired.

"*O'Malley?*" asked Scat.

"*O'Malley?*" asked the other cats.

Roquefort nodded furiously.

"Hold it, cats," said Scat. "This little guy is on the level!"

"You're darn tootin' right I'm on the level!" said Roquefort as he jumped off the cat's outstretched paw with as much dignity as he could muster.

"We didn't mean to rough you," one of the cats said gently, suddenly apologetic now that he knew Roquefort was a friend of O'Malley's.

76

"Don't worry about me!" said the mouse. "O'Malley needs help! Duchess and the kittens are in trouble!"

10

Edgar had dragged his sack containing Duchess and the kittens into the stable where he had hidden a big trunk. While Frou-Frou watched on in horror he threw the sack roughly into it and then slammed the lid shut. Inside the trunk the Aristocats whimpered with fear.

"Now, my pesky little pets, you're going to travel first class in your own private compartment!" he said as he secured the lid with a padlock.

He grinned as he read the destination label on the top of the trunk: *Timbuktu, French Equatorial Africa*.

"And this time you are never going to come back!"

Edgar bent down and began to push the trunk towards the stable door. There wasn't a moment to waste: he had already telephoned for the baggage van and it would be arriving soon. And then he would be rid of Duchess and her kittens for good; and Madame's millions would be his to inherit.

Suddenly several things happened at once.

O'Malley, who had managed to sneak into the stable, leapt onto Edgar, clawing at his face, and knocking him over the trunk. Before the butler had time to pick himself up, O'Malley rushed over and slammed the stable door shut.

Edgar rushed towards the door, but Frou-Frou stepped forward and grabbed Edgar's coat-tails in her mouth, pulling him back.

Angrily, Edgar wrenched his tail-coats away from the mare, and threw himself on the trunk, pushing it towards the door. From inside the trunk came the terrified screams of Duchess and her children.

O'Malley tried to prevent Edgar from reaching the door. He hissed and screeched at the butler, determined to save Duchess and the kittens from a life of misery on the other side of the world.

Edgar snarled and grabbed a pitchfork which had been left lying by a bale of hay in the corner of the stable. With hate burning in his eyes, he advanced upon O'Malley. Frou-Frou whinnied in terror.

He lunged at O'Malley and pinned him to the stable wall. He gave a laugh of triumph and then pushed the trunk to the door. Trapped against the wall, there was no way O'Malley could stop him.

Thinking of all the millions that would soon be his, Edgar opened the stable door, and shrieked in horror.

Scat Cat and his cronies were there, waiting for him. The alley cats burst in, knocking the butler to the floor, and started biting and scratching at him. As O'Malley struggled to free himself from the pitchfork, Roquefort jumped on top of the trunk and started work on its combination lock.

The sound of Edgar's screams and yelps of pain as the alley cats attacked him, and Frou-Frou's neighs of encouragement, were deafening.

"QUIET!" yelled Roquefort, as he listened for the fall of the tumblers in the combination lock. Everyone froze.

There was a tiny *click*! and Roquefort unlocked the combination lock. Everyone started fighting again.

O'Malley leapt into the trunk, and untied the neck of the sack in which Duchess and the others were imprisoned.

Suddenly Edgar broke free of the alley cats, rushed over to the trunk and slammed the lid shut again, this time trapping O'Malley as well as the others.

"You're going to Timbuktu, if it's the last thing I do!" he gloated.

Just then a huge bale of hay fell on his head. One of Scat's cats had winched the bale up using an overhead pulley and dropped the entire load on top of the butler. Edgar groaned and tried to stand up, only to have Scat Cat pour a pail of water over him.

As he fell over again, one of the cats grabbed a horse collar from the stable wall, and threw it around him, pinning his arms to his side. In a flash, they attached the pulley to the collar and, with Frou-Frou's help, started to winch Edgar high up into the air.

With a cry of triumph, O'Malley sprang out of the open trunk, followed by a relieved Duchess, Marie, Berlioz and Toulouse.

The trunk wasn't empty for long, however. As soon as O'Malley and the others had leapt out of it, Frou-Frou dropped Edgar into it, and the cats slammed the lid tightly shut. Then, using all their strength, they pushed it out into the yard where the baggage van was just pulling up.

O'Malley and Duchess smiled as they saw the two delivery men pick up the trunk and load it into their van—and take Edgar all the way to Timbuktu.

11

Madame smiled at Duchess and her kittens. It was such a relief to have them back, she decided; she even liked the new ginger tom who had befriended them. She wondered if he would like to stay with them in her big mansion; after all, the kittens seemed to like him, and he and Duchess got on with each other very well indeed.

"I think we should get on with the will now," said Monsieur Hautecourt, Madame's lawyer.

"Yes, of course," she said. "You know what to do."

Hautecourt nodded and drew a fine line through Edgar's name on the will.

"You know, Georges," Madame sighed, "if Edgar had only known about the will, I'm sure he would never have left . . ."

By her side, Duchess, O'Malley and the kittens exchanged a meaningful look. If only Madame knew!

Madame went over to stroke Duchess, who purred.

"Duchess, it's wonderful to have you all back," she

said, and then reached over and stroked O'Malley too. "And I think that this young man is very handsome too. Shall we keep him in the family?"

Duchess and the kittens all meowed their agreement; even O'Malley allowed himself a little purr of pleasure.

"Of course we will," continued Madame. "We need a man about the house!" She smiled as Duchess and O'Malley cuddled closer to each other. "And we must be sure to provide for their future little ones."

"Of course," said Hautecourt with a twinkle in his eyes. "The more the merrier!"

Suddenly Hautecourt heard a wonderful toe-tapping sound coming from the hall. The cats all rushed downstairs, and Roquefort, who had popped out of his hole in the skirting board to see what all the fuss was about, followed them down.

"What is that music, Adelaide?" asked Hautecourt as he ran down the stairs to the hall. "It sounds like a gang of swinging hepcats!"

"That's exactly what they are, Georges," said Madame. "They're the start of my new foundation—my home for all the alley cats of Paris."

They reached the foot of the stairs to see the jazziest, grooviest, most hip-hopping jam session there had ever been happening right in the middle of Madame's hall.

Scat Cat was blowing a mean tune on his horn,

while Berlioz was pounding out a hot melody on the piano. Roquefort was standing on the top of the piano conducting all the other cats, while O'Malley and Duchess hopped and bopped to the infectious music. Even Frou-Frou had come in from her stable, and was standing in the open doorway, nodding her head in time to the music.

Madame and Hautecourt grinned, and started to clap in time to the music. There was no doubt about it: these cats sure knew how to swing. As they watched Duchess and O'Malley, Marie, Berlioz and Toulouse all jive to the hot music, obviously having the time of their lives, the humans even felt a little jealous.

For a moment they both wished that they could be rocking on down with Scat Cat and his cronies, having the time of their lives.

After all, they said to each other, everybody wants to be a cat.

Robert Swindells

**"Faithful, fearless, full of fun,
Winter, summer, rain or sun,
One for five, and five for one –
THE OUTFIT!"**

*Meet The Outfit—Jillo, Titch, Mickey and Shaz. Share in
their adventures as they fearlessly investigate any mystery,
and injustice, that comes their way . . .*

Move over, Famous Five, The Outfit are here!

The Secret of Weeping Wood

In the first story of the series, The Outfit are determined
to discover the truth about the eerie crying, coming
from scary Weeping Wood. Is the wood really haunted?
Are The Outfit brave enough to find out?

We Didn't Mean To, Honest!

The marriage of creepy Kenneth Kilchaffinch to snooty
Prunella could mean that Froglet Pond, and all its
wildlife, will be destroyed. So it's up to The Outfit to
make sure the marriage is off . . . But how?

Kidnap at Denton Farm

Farmer Denton's new wind turbine causes a protest
meeting in Lenton, and The Outfit find themselves in
the thick of it. But a *kidnap* is something they didn't
bargain for, and now they face their toughest
challenge yet . . .

THE BABYSITTERS CLUB

Need a babysitter? Then call the Babysitters Club. Kristy Thomas and her friends are all experienced sitters. They can tackle any job from rampaging toddlers to a pandemonium of pets. To find out all about them, read on!

THE BABYSITTERS CLUB MYSTERIES

Our favourite Babysitters are super-sleuths too! Don't miss the new series of Babysitters Club Mysteries:

Mysteries coming soon:

No 1: Stacey and the Missing Ring
When Stacey's accused of stealing a valuable ring from a new family she's been sitting for, she's devastated – Stacey is *not* a thief! One way or another the Babysitters have *got* to find that ring and save the reputation of the Club . . . before it's too late!

No 2: Beware! Dawn
Just *who* is the mysterious "Mr X" who's been sending threatening notes to Dawn and phoning her while she's babysitting, *alone*? Dawn is determined to get to the bottom of this mystery, but she's *pretty* scared . . . what if she's in real danger?

Look out for:

No 3: Mallory and the Ghost Cat
No 4: Kristy and the Missing Child
No 5: Mary Anne and the Secret in the Attic
No 6: The Mystery at Claudia's House

BABYSITTERS LITTLE SISTER

Meet Karen Brewer, aged 6. Already known to Babysitters fans as Kristy's little sister, for the very first time she features in a series of her very own.